WALTER THE EDUCATOR'S FUNDAMENTALS DAY

Walter the Educator's Fundamentals Day

A THOUGHT-PROVOKING COLLECTIBLE SHORT STORY

Walter the Educator

Silent King Books

SILENT KING BOOKS

SKB

Registered Copyright ©2024. Walter the Educator.

All rights reserved. No part of this book may be reproduced in any manner whatsoever without written permission except in the case of brief quotations embodied in critical articles and reviews.

First Printing, 2024

Disclaimer
This book is a literary work; the story is not about specific persons, locations, situations, and/or circumstances unless mentioned in a historical context. Any resemblance to real persons, locations, situations, and/or circumstances is coincidental. This book is for entertainment and informational purposes only. The author and publisher offer this information without warranties expressed or implied. No matter the grounds, neither the author nor the publisher will be accountable for any losses, injuries, or other damages caused by the reader's use of this book. The use of this book acknowledges an understanding and acceptance of this disclaimer.

A worldwide global crisis is upon us. Due to a lack of educated and skilled workers, the world economy is struggling. Intellectuals fault social media and the digital culture that has dumbed down humanity. The blame has been put on parents. The government has implemented a BIG tax credit for all families whose kids can pass a fundamental math exam, which has been determined to be the building block for all learning. TODAY IS WALTER THE EDUCATOR'S FUNDAMENTALS DAY.

FUNDAMENTALS DAY

The dawn of Fundamentals Day broke over a world teetering on the brink of intellectual collapse. Across continents and time zones, families stirred, their homes filled with an anxious anticipation. The significance of this day had been etched into the fabric of society, driven by a desperate need to reverse a global crisis that threatened to unhinge the very foundations of civilization.

Walter the Educator's Fundamentals Day

Decades of neglect had brought humanity to this precipice. Social media, once a tool of connectivity and enlightenment, had morphed into an insidious agent of distraction and misinformation. Digital culture, with its ceaseless streams of memes and viral videos, had eroded the pillars of critical thinking and deep learning. Parents, too, had been swept away by this tide, unwittingly fostering an environment where superficiality thrived.

Walter the Educator's Fundamentals Day

In response to this intellectual decay, governments around the world had united in an unprecedented move. They introduced a sweeping policy: a $25,000 tax credit for any family whose children could pass a fundamental math exam. This exam, crafted by leading educators and mathematicians, was designed to assess core competencies deemed essential for all learning. Today, millions of children would face this test, their performance carrying not just personal stakes but the weight of societal hope.

Walter the Educator's Fundamentals Day

In a modest apartment in New York City, the Ramirez family prepared for the day with a mix of determination and dread. Twelve-year-old Miguel had been studying relentlessly for months. His parents, Maria and José, had sacrificed evenings and weekends to tutor him, their own schooling years behind them. The allure of the tax credit was strong—it could mean a new start, a way out of the financial hardships that had plagued them for years.

Walter the Educator's Fundamentals Day

Miguel sat at the kitchen table, his textbooks spread around him like a fortress. He reviewed equations and theorems, his fingers trembling slightly. The pressure was immense; the future of his family seemed to rest on his small shoulders.

"Miguel, remember what we talked about," Maria said, her voice steady but eyes betraying her anxiety. "It's not just about the money. This is your chance to show what you can do, to prove that you are capable."

Walter the Educator's Fundamentals Day

José nodded in agreement. "You've worked hard, mijo. Trust in yourself."

Thousands of miles away in Beijing, Li Wei's family was experiencing a similar morning. Li Wei, a bright and curious thirteen-year-old, had always excelled in math, but the stakes today felt overwhelmingly high. His parents had emphasized the importance of this day, not just for the financial incentive, but as a means to a better future in an increasingly uncertain world.

Walter the Educator's Fundamentals Day

"Li Wei, you are our pride," his father said, placing a reassuring hand on his son's shoulder. "Today, you show everyone what we already know."

Walter the Educator's Fundamentals Day

In every corner of the globe, similar scenes played out. In Mumbai, Aisha prepared under the watchful eyes of her grandparents. In Lagos, Chidi reviewed his notes one last time while his mother cooked breakfast. In Berlin, Hannah checked her calculator, her father reminding her to stay calm and focused.

Walter the Educator's Fundamentals Day

The examination centers were a hive of activity, filled with children and parents, invigilators and educators. The atmosphere was charged with a mixture of hope and trepidation.

Walter the Educator's Fundamentals Day

Governments had pulled out all the stops to ensure the tests were fair and secure, aware that this day was not just about assessing knowledge but about restoring faith in the future.

Walter the Educator's Fundamentals Day

At precisely 9:00 AM, the exams began. Silence fell over the halls as pencils scratched on paper, calculators beeped softly, and minds raced. For hours, the children poured their hearts into the test, tackling problems that demanded not just rote memorization but genuine understanding and logical reasoning.

Walter the Educator's Fundamentals Day

As the day wore on, the world waited. News outlets provided constant updates, featuring interviews with educators and analysts who discussed the broader implications of Fundamentals Day. Would this initiative mark the beginning of a renaissance in education, a turning point away from the distractions of digital triviality? Or would it reveal deeper flaws in a system already strained to its breaking point?

Walter the Educator's Fundamentals Day

In the Ramirez household, the clock seemed to move agonizingly slow. Maria and José paced nervously, imagining every possible outcome. When Miguel finally returned home, his face was pale but his eyes shone with a quiet confidence.

"How did it go?" Maria asked, holding her breath.

Walter the Educator's Fundamentals Day

"I think I did well, mamá," Miguel replied, a small smile breaking through his exhaustion. "I answered all the questions."

Walter the Educator's Fundamentals Day

Relief washed over his parents, mingled with a cautious optimism. Similar scenes played out in homes across the globe, as families embraced their children and awaited the results that would be announced in the coming days.

Walter the Educator's Fundamentals Day

In the aftermath of Fundamentals Day, the world held its collective breath. For some, the results brought joy and financial relief. For others, it was a wake-up call, a stark reminder of the work still needed. Governments pledged to build on this momentum, investing in education and supporting families in fostering environments that valued learning over superficial engagement.

Walter the Educator's Fundamentals Day

Intellectuals continued to debate the root causes and long-term solutions, but one thing was clear: Fundamentals Day had ignited a spark. It was a step towards reclaiming a world where knowledge and critical thinking were paramount, a world where the next generation could thrive and innovate, untethered from the digital mire that had once threatened to engulf them.

Walter the Educator's Fundamentals Day

As the sun set on this momentous day, a new dawn beckoned—a future where humanity, armed with wisdom and resilience, could once again aspire to its highest ideals.

Walter the Educator's Fundamentals Day

The Aftermath

Weeks after Fundamentals Day, the world remained gripped by the reverberations of the event. News anchors and pundits dissected the outcomes, while social media buzzed with stories of triumph and tales of disappointment. The test results had finally been tallied and the data analyzed, revealing a complex portrait of humanity's intellectual landscape.

Walter the Educator's Fundamentals Day

In the Ramirez household, the tension had given way to celebration. Miguel had passed the exam with flying colors, securing the much-needed tax credit for his family. The $25,000 infusion was a lifeline, offering not just financial relief but a sense of validation and hope. With the newfound resources, Maria and José could invest in further education for Miguel and his younger sister, Sofia, ensuring they were better prepared for the future.

Walter the Educator's Fundamentals Day

Across the globe, families like the Ramirezes celebrated similar victories. In Beijing, Li Wei's success bolstered his family's standing in their community, opening doors to elite educational opportunities. In Mumbai, Aisha's stellar performance was hailed as a triumph over adversity, inspiring her peers to pursue their studies with renewed vigor.

Walter the Educator's Fundamentals Day

However, the picture was not entirely rosy. In many homes, the results were less than ideal, sparking introspection and, in some cases, despair. Governments had anticipated this and swiftly moved to provide additional support, rolling out tutoring programs, educational grants, and community initiatives aimed at lifting those who had faltered.

Walter the Educator's Fundamentals Day

A Movement Begins

In the wake of Fundamentals Day, a grassroots movement began to take shape. Parents, educators, and concerned citizens rallied around the idea of reclaiming intellectual rigor.

Walter the Educator's Fundamentals Day

Workshops and seminars were organized, focusing on critical thinking, problem-solving, and the cultivation of a deeper engagement with learning. Schools started to reassess their curricula, emphasizing foundational skills and interdisciplinary approaches.

Walter the Educator's Fundamentals Day

The tech giants, long criticized for their role in the intellectual decline, responded with a mix of defensiveness and proactive measures. Some platforms introduced features to promote educational content, while others faced regulatory pressures to curb the spread of misinformation and mindless entertainment. A new breed of apps emerged, designed to foster learning and intellectual growth, garnering praise from educators and parents alike.

Walter the Educator's Fundamentals Day

The Ramirez Family's New Chapter

For the Ramirez family, the weeks following Miguel's success were transformative. The tax credit allowed them to move to a better neighborhood, closer to reputable schools and educational resources. Miguel enrolled in advanced math and science classes, his confidence growing with each passing day. Sofia, inspired by her brother's achievement, showed a newfound interest in her studies, often sitting with Miguel to learn from him.

Walter the Educator's Fundamentals Day

Maria and José, too, felt the ripple effects. They joined a local parents' group dedicated to supporting children's education, attending workshops and sharing their experiences. The group became a tight-knit community, providing not just educational support but emotional and social camaraderie.

Walter the Educator's Fundamentals Day

One evening, as the family gathered for dinner, Miguel shared an idea that had been brewing in his mind. "What if we start a tutoring center here in our neighborhood?" he suggested. "We could help other kids prepare for next year's exam, and it could be a way for all of us to give back."

Walter the Educator's Fundamentals Day

Maria and José exchanged glances, their faces lighting up with pride. "That's a wonderful idea, Miguel," José said. "We could use the tax credit to fund it, at least to get it started."

Walter the Educator's Fundamentals Day

Over the next few months, the Ramirezes worked tirelessly to bring Miguel's vision to life. They converted their garage into a makeshift classroom, gathering donated books and supplies from neighbors and local businesses. Word spread quickly, and soon, children from all over the neighborhood were attending the tutoring sessions.

Walter the Educator's Fundamentals Day

A Global Shift

The Ramirez family's initiative was not an isolated event. Around the world, similar grassroots efforts blossomed. In Lagos, Chidi's mother organized a community learning center, while in Berlin, Hannah's father started a mentorship program for young students. These local efforts began to interconnect, forming a global network of educational support and collaboration.

Walter the Educator's Fundamentals Day

Governments, recognizing the success of these grassroots movements, began to integrate them into broader national strategies. Policies were enacted to support community-driven educational initiatives, providing funding, resources, and professional guidance. The focus on foundational skills in math and science expanded to include critical thinking, creativity, and emotional intelligence, laying the groundwork for a more holistic approach to learning.

Walter the Educator's Fundamentals Day

Intellectual Renaissance

As these efforts took root, the world began to witness a resurgence of intellectual curiosity and innovation. Universities reported an increase in students pursuing degrees in science, technology, engineering, and mathematics (STEM). Research institutions flourished with new talent, and industries saw a rejuvenated workforce capable of tackling complex global challenges.

Walter the Educator's Fundamentals Day

Governments, recognizing the success of these grassroots movements, began to integrate them into broader national strategies. Policies were enacted to support community-driven educational initiatives, providing funding, resources, and professional guidance. The focus on foundational skills in math and science expanded to include critical thinking, creativity, and emotional intelligence, laying the groundwork for a more holistic approach to learning.

Walter the Educator's Fundamentals Day

Intellectual Renaissance

As these efforts took root, the world began to witness a resurgence of intellectual curiosity and innovation. Universities reported an increase in students pursuing degrees in science, technology, engineering, and mathematics (STEM). Research institutions flourished with new talent, and industries saw a rejuvenated workforce capable of tackling complex global challenges.

Walter the Educator's Fundamentals Day

The narrative around digital culture also began to shift. While social media and technology remained integral parts of daily life, there was a growing emphasis on using these tools for meaningful engagement and education. Platforms that prioritized quality content over quantity gained popularity, and users became more discerning about how they spent their time online.

Walter the Educator's Fundamentals Day

Legacy of Fundamentals Day

Years later, the impact of Fundamentals Day was still palpable. It had sparked a global movement that redefined the value of education and intellectual growth. The lessons learned from that pivotal day continued to shape policies and practices, ensuring that future generations were better equipped to navigate the complexities of an ever-changing world.

Walter the Educator's Fundamentals Day

For the Ramirez family, the journey had come full circle. Miguel, now a renowned mathematician, often reflected on the day that had changed his life. He continued to run the tutoring center, now a well-established institution that had helped countless children realize their potential. Sofia, inspired by her brother and the community around her, pursued a career in education, dedicated to fostering the same sense of hope and opportunity that had once been given to her.

Walter the Educator's Fundamentals Day

As the world looked towards the future, the legacy of Fundamentals Day served as a reminder of the power of collective action and the enduring importance of education. It was a testament to what could be achieved when societies united to uplift their youngest members, ensuring that the flame of knowledge burned bright for generations to come.

Walter the Educator's Fundamentals Day

ABOUT THE CREATOR

Walter the Educator is one of the pseudonyms for Walter Anderson. Formally educated in Chemistry, Business, and Education, he is an educator, an author, a diverse entrepreneur, and he is the son of a disabled war veteran. "Walter the Educator" shares his time between educating and creating. He holds interests and owns several creative projects that entertain, enlighten, enhance, and educate, hoping to inspire and motivate you.

> Follow, find new works, and stay up to date
> with Walter the Educator™
> at WaltertheEducator.com

www.ingramcontent.com/pod-product-compliance
Lightning Source LLC
LaVergne TN
LVHW051922060526
838201LV00060B/4134